dick bruna

miffy at the seaside

SIMON AND SCHUSTER
London New York Sydney Toronto New Delhi

One day Father Bunny said,

who wants to come with me?

I'm going where the sandy dunes

roll down to meet the sea.

Oh yes! said Miffy. I'll come too.

I like the beach a lot.

I'll take my bucket with me

as my shell-collecting pot.

Good, said Father. In you hop.

I'll pull you in the cart.

It's quick and not too tiring for you.

That's the way to start.

Father, aren't the sand dunes high?

called Miffy in surprise.

Then Father pointed. Look, the beach!

Right before our eyes.

They stopped beside a stripy tent.

Miffy, look, we're here.

Thanks for pulling me so well,

said Miffy with a cheer.

Then Miffy put her costume on

and stood there waiting in it.

Goodness! Father Bunny said.

You didn't waste a minute.

To make a castle now you'll need

your bucket and your spade.

Later on we'll test it

to see how well it's made.

Miffy dug with all her strength.

Her fort began to rise

till all that you could see of her

was just her ears and eyes.

When little Miffy's fort was made

she walked beside the sea.

She filled her bucket up with shells.

How pretty they could be!

Then Miffy was allowed to go

with Father for a swim.

He didn't seem to mind when Miffy

started splashing him.

But after they had dried themselves

Father Bunny said,

it's time that we were heading home,

my little sleepy head.

Oh no, cried Miffy. I'm not tired.

I'm wide awake and bright.

But as they trundled homeward

her eyes were closing tight.

original title: nijntje aan zee
Original text Dick Bruna © copyright Mercis Publishing bv, 1963
Illustrations Dick Bruna © copyright Mercis bv, 1963
This edition published in Great Britain in 2015 by Simon and Schuster UK Limited,
Publication licensed by Mercis Publishing bv, Amsterdam
English translation by Tony Mitton, 2015
ISBN 978-1-4711-2334-4
Printed and bound in China
All rights reserved, including the right of reproduction in whole or in part in any form
A CIP catalogue record for this book is available from the British Library upon request
10 9 8 7 6 5 4 3 2

www.simonandschuster.co.uk